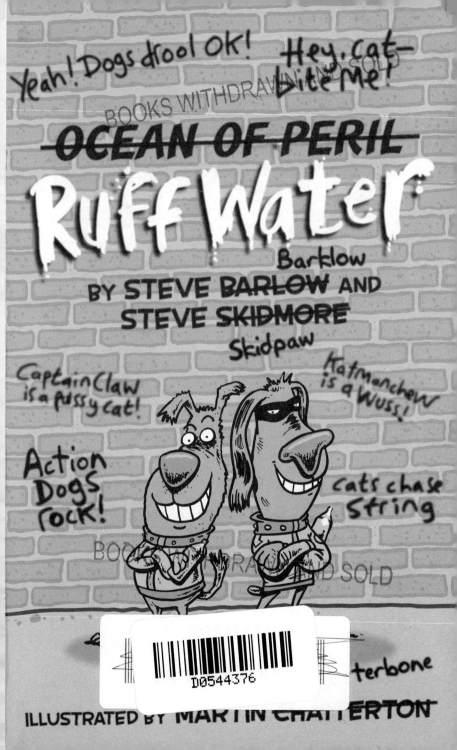

WHO ARE THE ACTION DOGS?

FOR THOUSANDS OF YEARS, DOGS HAVE BEEN MAN'S BEST FRIEND.

THEY HAVE HELPED US HUNT FOR OUR FOOD.

THEY HAVE LOOKED AFTER OUR ANIMALS AND GUARDED OUR HOMES.

THEY HAVE HELPED POLICE TO TRACK DOWN CRIMINALS.

THEY HAVE RESCUED PEOPLE LOST IN THE SNOW, OR BURIED BY EARTHQUAKES.

BUT IN THE TWENTY-FIRST CENTURY, THE WORLD HAS BECOME MUCH MORE COMPLICATED.

OUR HOMES ARE GUARDED BY BURGLAR ALARMS AND CCTV.

WE BUY FOOD FROM THE SUPERMARKET INSTEAD OF CHASING IT.

WE HAVE SPECIAL HEAT-SEEKING CAMERAS TO FIND MISSING PEOPLE.

HUMAN BEINGS HAVE BECOME A LOT CLEVERER...

SO HAVE DOGS!

AND WHEN DANGER THREATENS, IT'S TIME TO UNLEASH THE. . .

SPIKE
TOP DOG

YAPPER
THE ACTION DOGS'
EYES AND EARS

MASTER YI
TAEKWONDOG
MASTER

The cat sat on the mat.

The cat didn't want to be there. He was shaking. Not from the cold or snow that was settling on his fur, but from fear...fear at the thought of his master, who was waiting on the other side of the cat flap.

And most of all, fear at how his master would receive the news he brought.

The cat tried to remember how many of his nine lives he had used up…just in case. He took a deep breath and stretched out a claw to scratch at the flap.

The deep voice echoed around the secret valley, causing several minor avalanches on the snow-covered mountain slopes.

The cat gulped. How did his master know he was outside? Trembling with fear, he bolted through the cat flap, which went *flapalapaflapalapa laplaplap* behind him.

MASTER KATMANCHEW,
I BRING NEWS OF YOUR BRILLIANTLY FIENDISH PLAN TO STEAL ALL THE GOLD FROM THE VAULTS OF THE WORLD BANK...(GULP!)

Katmanchew let out a screech of rage. "Those do-gooding pests! I hate the Action Dogs!" His paw slammed down on a button and the floor opened up beneath the unfortunate messenger, who briefly remembered how many lives he had used up: all nine.

As the slabs of the floor rose back into their usual place, Katmanchew leaned back on his throne. "Katnip?" he called. "Where are you, my faithful servant?"

Benji stood at the bus stop outside the downtown dog shelter, reading his newspaper.

Benji loved reading about the Action Dogs. Their brave deeds and incredible machines had made them world famous. No one knew who the Action Dogs were, or where they came from. But when humans needed help, they were always there, saving people from terrible danger and making criminals wished they'd stayed in bed.

They certainly seem to lead exciting lives, thought Benji. *More exciting than mine, anyway. I wish I could be like them!*

That's a bit rude, thought Benji. *I'll show them.*
He picked up the ball. "Here it comes," he called.

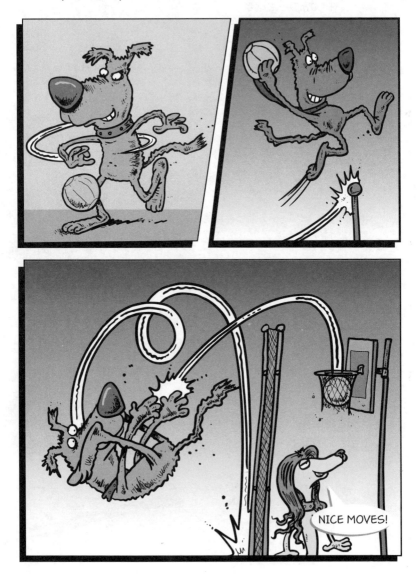

Benji dropped to the ground and brushed himself down. The dogs in the pound stared at him in amazement. He felt quite pleased with himself, especially when a pretty Afghan hound came over for a chat.

Benji shuddered. "Fleas! Yeuch! Only stray dogs get fleas."

Sally shrugged. "I'm a stray. That's why I'm in here."

"Oh, I didn't mean all strays," said Benji quickly. "I mean, I'm sure you haven't got fleas..." He tailed off and gave Sally a hangdog look. "Me and my big muzzle."

"Don't worry about it," said Sally cheerfully.

"It must be rough in there," said Benji, trying to change the subject. "I guess you don't get out much."

Sally gave him a grin. "Oh, you'd be surprised. So – you're not a stray then?"

Benji shook his head. "I'm a night watchdog at the docks," he said proudly. "And that's my bus," he added as a bus pulled up at the stop.

Benji took his seat, and the bus moved off.

Sally watched the bus pull away. "Did you see the way he moved with that ball? We could use somebody with that kind of skill."

The Dobermann called Spike scratched his ear with his paw. "He's just a mutt. Forget him."

"You never know," said Sally. "I've got a feeling
we might see him again – very soon..."

"You got the paper, Benji? Good dog!"

Benji looked up at Old Fred's call. He ran across the dockside to the night watchman.

THIS HERE SHIP IS CARRYING SPECIAL TOP-SECRET EQUIPMENT. VERY HUSH HUSH.

Benji dropped his newspaper at Old Fred's feet and the watchman glanced at the headlines. "Action Dogs, eh? We could do with them round here tonight."

Benji barked excitedly.

"No, not 'Woof woof' – 'Hush hush'!" Old Fred chuckled. "Anyway, your job is to guard this ship, the MS *Retriever*. If you see anyone *acting suspicious* – lurking in shadows, that style of thing – you just bark and I'll come running."

Benji barked again.

"That's right," said Old Fred. "Just like that." He rubbed Benji's ears. "Good boy."

Benji trotted to the bottom of the gangplank that led from the dock to the ship and sat down. It was dark. The new moon cast deep pools of shadow.

Benji took his duties very seriously. Most watchdogs would have found a cosy corner to curl up in. Not Benji. He looked all around, but he couldn't see anyone *acting suspicious*. So he stood up and started marching up and down in front of the gangplank. Five paces to the right...then five to the left...then back again.

Benji was so busy marching, he didn't notice that he was being watched by many pairs of eyes. He didn't notice the nimble-footed shapes that slid from shadow to shadow. He didn't notice the almost-silent padding of paws as they rushed across the dockside towards him.

But he did notice...

CATS! AAAARGHHHH!

Benji tried to bark, to warn Old Fred. But he only managed a sort of strangled yelp before one of the cats stuffed a ball of wool into his mouth.

Benji closed his eyes and waited for the blow – but it never came.

Instead, there was a furious yowling. The biggest, meanest-looking cat Benji had ever seen appeared out of nowhere. He leaped on the cat who had threatened Benji and struck him to the ground.

The ginger cat pointed at Benji. "Tie the mutt
up and carry him on board. Prepare to go to sea!"
Benji struggled fiercely, but the cats held
him firm. They tied ropes around him, pulling
the knots really tight, and grinning when
Benji yelped with pain. Then
they lifted him up like a sack
of flour and carried him up
the gangplank of the
MS *Retriever*.

YOU'RE OUR PRISONER.
THINK YOURSELF LUCKY.
IT'S A RARE HONOUR TO BE
CAPTURED BY ME – CAPTAIN CLAW –
LOYAL FOLLOWER OF THE MIGHTY
KATMANCHEW – THE EMPEROR OF
CRIME AND THE WICKEDEST CAT
IN THE WORLD!

They've started the engines! They're going to steal the ship! Benji groaned. *I bet no watchdog has ever lost a whole ship before!* he thought bitterly.

The engines were going faster as the ship got under way. Benji watched in despair as the cranes on the dockside slid by. He heard a distant shout as Old Fred ran out of his hut waving his arms. Benji wanted to bark a warning to him. He managed to spit out the gag – but it was too late!

"Now, puppy," snarled Captain Claw, "I suppose you're wondering why we've gone and stolen this ship. Well, Katmanchew says it's full of new equipment for the Action Dogs! And now we've stolen it, all their secrets will be ours!"

Benji's heart sank as the cats cheered. His heroes were going to lose the amazing inventions they needed to mount their daring rescues, and it would be all his fault!

"But there's no need for you to be worrying yourself about that, puppy," growled Captain Claw, "because you won't be around to see it. As soon as we're out of sight of land, we're going to make you walk the plank!"

Benji shuddered. He'd heard legends of the dreaded Gravy Bones, who drove poor sea dogs mad with promises of delicious treats. The hungry dogs would throw themselves into the sea to drown, and be dragged down to Gravy Bones's Locker. It looked as if he would be joining them, any time now.

He glanced down. There were nasty-looking triangular fins cutting though the water far below. Sharks!

Benji gritted his teeth. He wasn't going to let the cats know he was afraid. He glared at them.

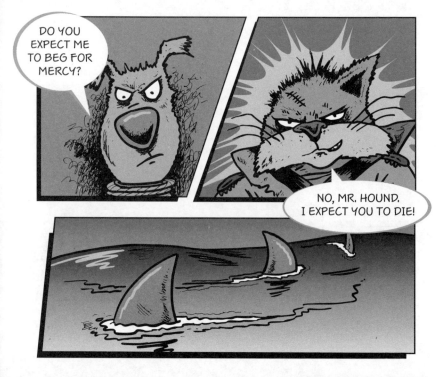

Suddenly, the cats' jeering stopped. Benji looked up in surprise, and saw another vessel heading across the dark water straight for the *Retriever*. It was moving very fast. The cats began yowling, caterwauling and waving their fists at it.

IT'S THE *DOG PADDLE!* BACK TO YOUR STATIONS, YOU COWARDLY SWABS. FULL SPEED AHEAD! THE ACTION DOGS ARE ON OUR TAILS!

"The Action Dogs," gasped Benji. "They must be coming to rescue me!" But his relief didn't last long. The ship gave a jerk that nearly threw him off the plank. Its propellers churned the sea, and it started to move. Slowly at first, then faster and faster...

But the other ship was faster still. It shot through the water like an arrow, making straight for the *Retriever* – nearer and nearer...

"Hard a' starboard!" yelled Captain Claw. The ship began to turn.

The movement threw Benji off his feet. He landed face down on the plank and rolled from side to side as the *Retriever* pitched and tossed in the waves. Moments later, the ship gave a powerful lurch. With a howl of despair, Benji toppled off the plank – and suddenly found himself dangling upside down.

Benji held on for as long as he could. But his legs were slipping. Centimetre by centimetre... bit by bit... He braced himself for the cold of the water and the sharp teeth of the sharks.

HOPE THOSE SHARKS DON'T LIKE DOG FOOD. AND IF THEY DO EAT ME, I HOPE I MAKE THEM REALLY, REALLY SICK!

But he didn't hit the water. The boat that been chasing the *Retriever* had finally caught up.

Benji sat up. His head was spinning. Everything looked blurred. Someone bent over him. It looked like the pretty hound he'd met at the shelter. But no, it couldn't be...

Benji looked up into the pretty Afghan's eyes. His head was swimming, but at least the rest of him wasn't. He tried to say something brave and clever, but all that came out was, "Sure thing. never better." Then he passed out.

When Benji came to, he found himself in a bright room. The light made his head hurt.

Benji tried to sit up, and let out a whine of pain.

"Feeling sore, are you?" said the girl. "I'm not surprised. You've had a nasty bump on the head." She lifted Benji down from the table. "I'm Janet. I'm the kennelmaid around here. You can stay until you're feeling better. In the meantime, Sally can show you around – can't you, Sally?" She bustled about putting bandages and scissors away.

Sally gave Benji a friendly grin. "Come on."

Benji stared at her. Suddenly, everything came back to him. The Action Dogs – they had caught up with the cats and rescued him. "You were on the ship," he said excitedly. "The one that chased after Captain Claw and his gang!

Sally looked uncomfortable. "Maybe that bump on your head is making you see things..."

Benji shook his head, and wished he hadn't: it hurt a lot. "It *was* you," he insisted. "But if you aren't with the Action Dogs, how did I get here?"

"The Action Dogs brought you here," Sally told him. "They said it was the closest place they could think of where you could get treatment."

"Well, I guess that makes sense," said Benji grudgingly. "But you still haven't told me what you were doing on the ship that rescued me."

Sally shrugged. "Well, then, why not just forget the whole thing and wait for a nice foster-family to come and claim you?"

But Benji was feeling stubborn. "No," he said. "I know it was you on that ship! I'm not leaving until I find out what really happened, and who you really are."

Sally sighed. "I was afraid you'd feel that way." She stopped outside a kennel, reached inside, and pulled out a bone.

Benji stared at Sally. She was talking to a bone. The poor girl was clearly barking mad!

Sally caught the stare. "It's all right," she said. "I'm not crazy. This is a bone phone. It's how we stay in touch. Let's go." She led the way into a kennel.

Feeling confused, Benji followed. Sally pushed a
large button on the back wall.

The evil crime lord scratched at the arms of his throne. His claws left deep grooves in the polished wood. "Worthless fool! You bring me nothing but a *katalogue* of disaster – and you know the penalty for failure!"

HAVE THIS MISERABLE HALFWIT FLAYED ALIVE WITH THE KAT-O'-NINE-TAILS!

IT SHALL BE DONE, O MERCIFUL ONE!

SPARE ME!

Two burly hench-cats seized the terrified Claw and dragged him, sobbing and pleading, from the room. They had almost reached the door when...

The evil mastermind rubbed his chin in thought. "There may be one way in which this useless creature can make amends for his mistakes, and save his miserable skin..."

Sally nudged Benji. "Spike didn't want me to tell you anything. Don't let him get to you," she whispered.

Spike gave Benji an angry look, and turned to Sally. "You know I think this is a bad idea," he growled.

"It's better that he knows the truth," said Sally. "I'm sure he'll keep quiet about us when he understands how important it is that we stay a secret organization."

"Says you!" Spike pointed a paw at Benji. "What's to stop the big-mouthed mutt blabbing to everybody when he leaves here?"

There was a shocked silence. Then Spike burst out laughing. "You?"

Benji's hackles rose. "Yes – why not? What's wrong with me?"

"You got yourself kidnapped by a bunch of flea-bitten cats," barked Spike. "And you call yourself a dog? You're pathetic!"

Benji was furious. "Go sniff a lamp post, big shot!" He prepared to launch himself at Spike.

51

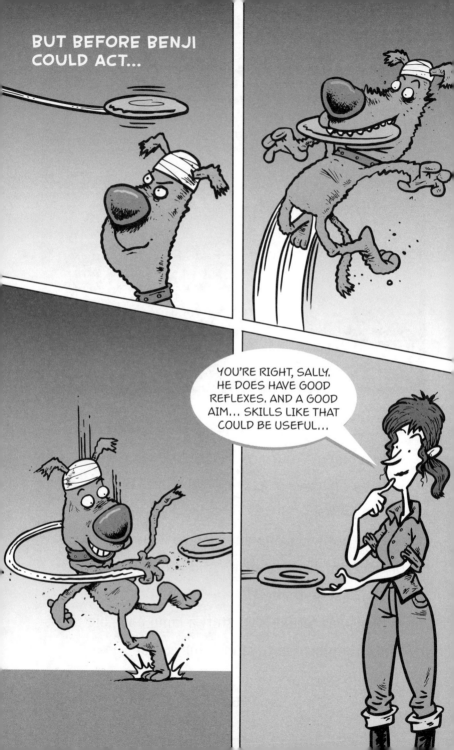

"Janet!" said Spike angrily. "You can't even be thinking about letting this no-hoper join us."

"Calm down, Spike," said Janet. "Come and tell me about what happened on the mission."

Benji's mouth dropped wide open. He looked from Spike to Janet and back again. "She understood what he just said! How can that be? Dogs can understand humans, but humans can't understand dogs. Humans aren't very bright."

Janet laughed. "Don't worry, Benji. Spike, tell me how you got the gear from the *Retriever* back here..." She and Spike walked away.

Benji turned to Sally. "What *did* happen on the mission? How did you know the cats had stolen the ship?"

"The night watchman called the police and the coastguard," Sally told him. "We listened in on the call. Then we came looking for you in the *Dog Paddle* – it's the fastest thing afloat," she added proudly.

"Can I see it?" Benji asked eagerly.

Sally laughed. "Later. Come and meet the gang."

9 THE DOGJO

THIS IS THE DOGJO. IT'S WHERE WE DO OUR TRAINING.
TRAINING? FOR WHAT?
FOR FIGHTING KATMANCHEW'S CATS, WHEN WE HAVE TO. THEY'RE TRAINED IN KATRATE, BUT WE'RE ALL EXPERTS IN THE ANCIENT MARTIAL ART OF TAEKWONDOG.

"I'd like to learn that!" Benji pointed at the old Pekingese. "Who's he? Is he asleep?"

"That is Master Yi Sun Kwan. He is our instructor. And he isn't asleep, he's meditating."

Benji gave a disbelieving chortle. "He's a martial arts expert? You're kidding!"

Sally glared at him. "Why do you say that?"

"Because he's as old as the hills and knee-high to a Dachshund!"

The old Pekingese opened his eyes. He rose

gracefully to his feet and bowed to Benji. "Size, everything is not," he said mildly. "You wish to learn, my impetuous young friend?"

Despite his amazing reflexes, Benji never even saw the old dog move.

ARRRRRRGGGHHH!

Benji scrambled to his feet and bowed as low as he could. "I am sorry, Master Yi," he said. "Please, will you teach me?"

The old Pekingese looked steadily at Benji. "Maybe," he said at last. "First, patience you must learn." He sank to the floor and closed his eyes again as if nothing had happened.

Sally gave Benji a rueful smile. "Come on. Let's see what's happening at the Listening Post."

Benji found himself in a room full of radar screens, TV monitors, computers, recording devices and a number of machines whose purpose he couldn't even guess at.

"A fire downtown," Yapper went on, "but they got everyone out of the building. A couple of car wrecks, but nobody hurt bad. Some hoods robbed a jewellery store but the police caught them."

"Sounds like Katmanchew's lying low for the moment, then." Sally gave Yapper a friendly pat on the back. "Nothing there for us. Keep listening."

"Sure," said Yapper, his eyes never leaving the screens.

"Yapper keeps his eyes and ears on world communications," Sally told Benji as they left the room. "His job is to listen out for distress calls that only the Action Dogs can handle – and anything Katmanchew might be involved in. Right, it's time you met Rascal and Murdoch."

A cross-looking Scottie glanced up from his work. "That's easy for ye to say," he growled. "I work my paws to the bone building marvels of engineering, just so irresponsible ruffians like you and Spike can go out and ruin them. And then ye have the nerve to complain about how long it takes me to do the repairs! I'm not a miracle worker!" The Scottie disappeared back into the engine compartment, from which rose the sounds of muttering and the rattle of spanners. These were followed by a muffled voice. "Try the starter again!"

Grinning, Rascal pressed the starter.

Rascal chuckled as the Scottish terrier dived back under the vehicle's bonnet.

Benji gawped. "What an amazing machine." He pointed at Murdoch's wriggling bottom. "Did he really build it?"

Sally gave him a grin and nodded. "Yep – he's incredible. Look – here are the plans for Rover."

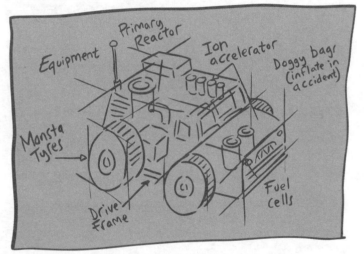

"We use Rover for local rescues," explained Sally. "But we're the Action Dogs, remember. If we have to go further, we have other machines."

Rascal climbed down from the cab and gave Benji a friendly grin. "That's the truth, so listen well. Now's the time to show and tell!"

11 THE ACTION STATION

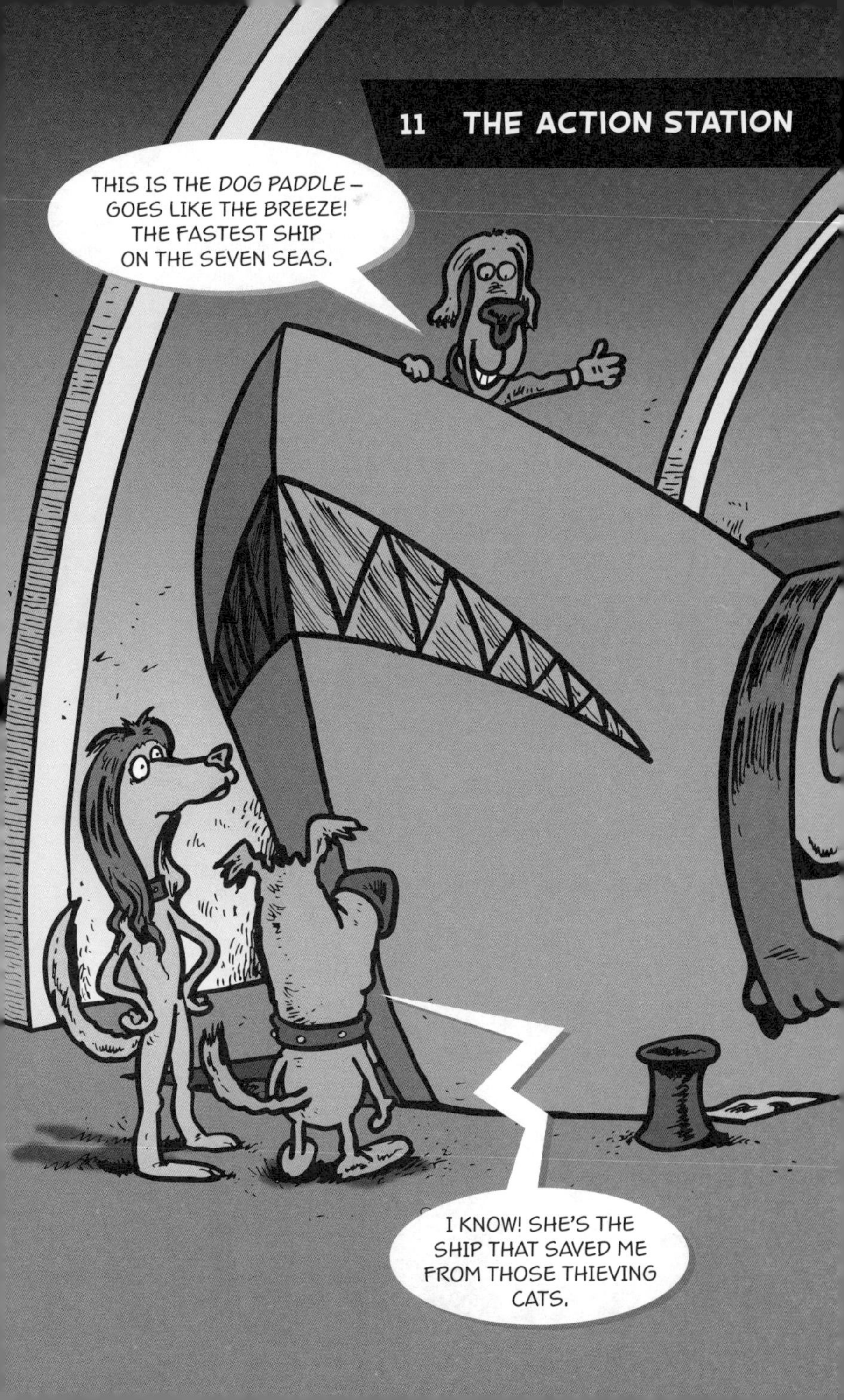

Sally laughed. "What Rascal means is, it carries all the heavy equipment we need for a rescue."

"What sort of equipment?" asked Benji.

Sally thought for a moment. "Well, for instance..."

Sally gave Rascal an enquiring glance. "Haven't you got anything to say about this one?"

Rascal shook his head. "Guess I'll let it go this time. 'Maxileash' ain't got no rhyme."

Sally laughed. "Anyway, we're lucky we still have this. It was on the *Retriever* when she was hijacked. Katmanchew would love to get his claws on our equipment."

Benji stared at the Maxileash. "It looks like a giant dog lead."

"That's pretty much what it is," agreed Sally. "It fires like a harpoon, but it has a powerful clamp on the end – like a dog collar. We should be able to tow almost anything with it. Would you like to see the Flying Frisbee?"

Benji licked his lips. "I'd love to see—" But he was interrupted by a loud barking noise from the tannoy system.

Benji bounced up and down in excitement. "What is it?" he yapped. "A dangerous rescue? Katmanwotsit up to some evil scheme?"

Sally groaned. "It's worse that that! It's Welfare Officer Brick!"

Several confusing seconds later, Benji found himself in a line of dogs in the yard of the dog shelter.

"What's going on?" he asked in a dazed voice.

"Just stand still," hissed Sally. "It's an inspection."

Spike gave them an angry look. "No talking in the ranks," he snapped. Then he glanced down the row and barked, "Tennn-hun!"

At once, all the dogs in the yard sat stiffly to attention, their muzzles in the air. Hurriedly, Benji did the same.

A door opened and Janet the kennelmaid came out into the yard. She had someone else with her.

As the man moved down the line making notes on his clipboard, Sally whispered to Benji, "That's Welfare Officer Brick. He's a real pain. I think he suspects there's something going on here that he doesn't know about."

Benji grinned. "I'll say there is!"

Sally laughed. "Right! But he's Janet's boss, so whenever he comes snooping we have to be on our best behaviour or she'd be in trouble. And of course, we can't launch a rescue mission when he's around."

"What's this?" Welfare Officer Brick's voice was sharp. He was further down the line, staring at Murdoch. "What's that on this dog's nose, Miss Goodenough? It looks like gravy."

Murdoch hadn't switched on his dog-collar translator, so Welfare Officer Brick didn't understand a word of this. He stepped back in alarm and pointed at Murdoch. "He growled at me! You heard him – he growled at me!" He made a note on his clipboard.

Janet gave Murdoch an angry look. "I'm sure he didn't mean it, sir."

Welfare Officer Brick wagged his finger at her. "You know the rules! No doggie treats in this shelter. Especially for bad dogs who growl at people! Hard biscuits and water for this lot."

"That's not Yapper!" hissed Benji. "Where is he?"

"Sssh!" said Sally. "He can't leave the Listening Post, so we made a fake Yapper to fool Welfare Officer Brick."

Before the inspection was over, Benji felt quite trembly from sitting to attention. At last Janet managed to get rid of Officer Brick and Benji could relax with a sigh. But seconds later, he pricked up his ears as another rapid series of barks sounded from the loudspeakers in every kennel.

"This is a recording of a distress call," said Yapper. He tapped at his computer keyboard.

"*Mayday, mayday!*" The frightened voice echoed round the Action Station. "*This is the cruise liner* Dontpanic. *We are being hijacked by a bunch of ca-*aaargh!"

Benji whispered to Sally, "What are ca-aaarghs?"

"He's trying to say 'cats'," hissed Sally. "Katmanchew's gang, I bet. They must have jumped him as he made the call."

"Oh, yeah. Right," said Benji sheepishly.

THE *DONTPANIC* – ISN'T THAT THE REVOLUTIONARY NUCLEAR-POWERED CRUISE SHIP?

THAT'S RIGHT. IT'S ON ITS MAIDEN VOYAGE, AND IT'S IN BIG TROUBLE.

"I've picked up some more details by listening to mobile phone calls from the ship," continued Yapper. "It seems Captain Claw and his cats have taken over the *Dontpanic* and they're ransacking the passengers' cabins for loot."

"Captain Claw," snarled Spike. "I bet Katmanchew is behind this."

"That's not all," said Yapper. "They've also destroyed the computer that controls the ship's course and its engines. It's travelling at full speed and it's impossible to steer."

"We have to stop that ship!" said Janet. "Sandy Banks is our most popular holiday playground. The beaches will be full of people having fun."

Sally was horrified. "When the *Dontpanic* hits the island, the engines will explode, destroying everything. All the holidaymakers will be blown to smithereens – along with all the ship's passengers and crew. We must save them!"

Murdoch shook his head. "They hav'nae a dog's chance. It cannae be done."

Sally rolled her eyes. "Murdoch, you're always saying things like that. We can fly you to the ship, and you can shut the engines down. We all know what a genius you are..."

"I may be a genius," barked Murdoch, "but I cannae change the laws of physics! I know how those nuclear engines work. It takes two hours to shut them down – and at that speed, the ship will crash into the island in one hour."

Even as Murdoch was predicting disaster, on the far side of the world the faithful Katnip bowed low before his evil master.

Katmanchew pressed a hidden button on his throne, which turned in a half-circle.

The crime lord's eyes glowed with an unholy light. "And you have carried out your orders?"

Captain Claw grovelled until his nose brushed the deck. "All of them, most evil master. To the letter."

"Excellent." Katmanchew gestured, and the screen went dark. The furry master-criminal leaned back in his throne with a contented sigh.

"Behold my evil genius, Katnip," he said softly. "Captain Claw has sabotaged the *Dontpanic*. The Action Dogs will try to save the ship, and be blown to pieces when its engines explode."

Katnip bowed again. "Master, truly your wickedness knows no bounds."

Katmanchew could contain his glee no longer – he exploded from his throne.

Spike gave the others a determined look. "All right, here's what we do. We use the *Dog Paddle* to push the *Dontpanic* off course so it'll miss Sandy Banks."

Murdoch scowled. "That won't work. The *Paddle* is no' powerful enough to move a great big ship like that."

"Couldn't we take the passengers off with the Bonecopter?" suggested Sally.

Yapper shook his head. "There's not enough time.

And what about the people on Sandy Banks? They'd never get away."

Benji raised his paw.

"Excuse me," he said shyly. "I think I have an idea."

"You're not part of the team," growled Spike.

"I think we should hear what Benji has to say," said Janet kindly. "Well, Benji?"

Benji shuffled his paws. "It's just that...well, I went to a dog show once..."

Spike stared at him. "You were entered in a dog show? What as?"

Benji muttered, "Dog with the waggiest tail." Spike gave a bark of laughter. "Anyway," said Benji hurriedly, "the show was in a dance hall and the floor was really slippery. There was one lady with a very small dog. She was walking it for the judges, but when she stopped the dog's claws wouldn't grip, so it kept going."

Spike yawned. "What has this got to do with anything?"

"I just thought," said Benji, "when Sally showed me the Maxileash..."

"Hot dog!" Sally jumped up from her seat. "I think he's got it!"

HERE'S THE PLAN. WE FIX THE MAXILEASH ON THIS LITTLE ISLAND AND FIRE IT AT THE SHIP.

Sally continued, "So the Maxileash pulls the ship around the island like the little dog's leash pulled it around its owner. That will move the ship away from Sandy Banks. The Maxileash is on a swivel, so the *Dontpanic* will just keep going round the island like a satellite orbiting the earth until Murdoch and Rascal shut down the engines."

Rascal whistled. "That'll do it – never fear. The dude done had a doozie idea!"

"Right!" Spike took command.

Spike stared at Yapper. "What about you?"

"Get me to the ship," said Yapper excitedly, "and I'll fight all those cats single-pawed and chase them off! Or how about I fly the Bonecopter – or fix the Maxileash? I can abseil down a rope and—"

"Sorry, Yapper," said Janet kindly. "We need you here to handle communications between the teams."

Yapper's face fell. "Awwww, I never have any fun."

I COULD USE A PAW FIXING THE MAXILEASH...

I CAN DO IT! LET ME!

Spike glared at Benji. "I told you before..."

"Oh, come on, Spike," said Sally. "You said yourself we could use some help. And it *is* Benji's idea."

Janet nodded. "Sally's right. Benji, you can help." Benji turned a somersault with delight.

"All right," growled Spike. "It's time to unleash the Action Dogs! F.I.D.O.!"

F.I.D.O.!

RIGHT!

"Where does the tunnel go?" asked Benji.

Sally wrinkled her nose. "Into the main sewer. That's how it gets away from here without being seen. The sewer outfall opens right out onto the bay."

Back in the Action Station, Spike stuck his head into the Bonecopter's equipment bay. "Are you two going to chew the fat all day, or shall we get going?"

Sally and Benji hurried to their seats.

EVERYONE READY?

Benji looked worried. "Do we have to go through the sewers, too?"

Sally turned in her seat and gave him a wink. "No. We leave straight from the shelter."

"But won't anyone see us take off?"

"Not a chance. You know how often fog rolls in off the bay?" Benji nodded. "Well, sometimes we give it a little help."

Sally spoke into her microphone. "Bonecopter to Yapper. We're on our way. Hey, Yapper? Give us some smoke for take-off please."

Benji gave a cry of delight. "Here we go – my first mission. Yappee!"

Benji twisted and turned in his seat, trying to look out of every window at the same time. "We're flying!" he yapped.

Spike rolled his eyes. "No kidding!"

Benji gave Spike an apologetic look. "Sorry – I guess this is all just routine to you. But I've never flown before."

Sally reached for a button. "Switching to supersonic mode."

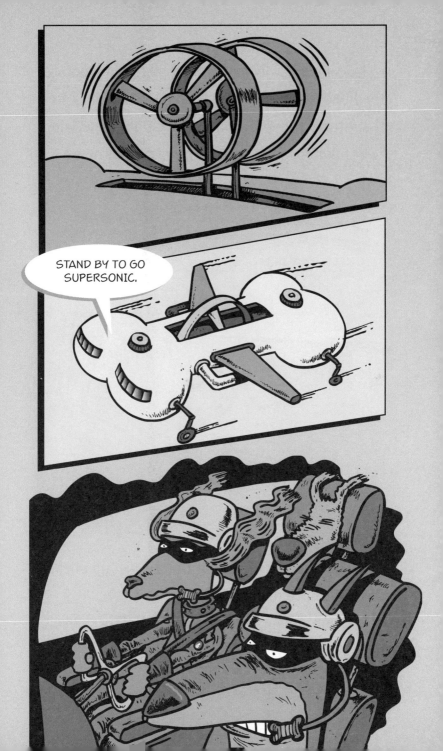

It seemed hardly any time at all to Benji before the Bonecopter slowed as Sally switched back to the rotors. "If my calculations are right," she said, "we should be over the *Dontpanic* about now."

Sally nodded. "The Isle of Dogs is just up ahead. We don't have much time."

"All right, team," said Spike briskly. "Let's get to work."

They landed with a jolt on the top of the island.
Benji unclipped his safety belt and stepped away
from the Maxileash, feeling a bit wobbly. Being
winched down from the Bonecopter had been kind
of fun, but also pretty scary.

Spike cast off the winch line and spoke into his dogtooth radio. "Okay, Sally. We're down. Winch in the cable and stand off. We're going to fix the Maxileash."

Sally's reply sounded squeakily from the radio's speaker. "*F.I.D.O.*"

"F.I.D.O?" said Benji. "What does that mean?"

"It means 'Okay'," said Spike. He opened his tool case. "Lucky there's good solid rock here. We need a strong platform to fire the clamp."

Benji did
as he was
told, but the
noise of the gun
was very loud,
and Benji jumped
every time Spike fired
it to send strong
bolts down into the rock.

Spike put the gun to one side. "Now, pass me the bulldogs."

Benji looked blank. "What sort of dogs?"

"Not real dogs," said Spike impatiently. "Bulldog clips. Those clippy things there. Sheesh."

"Er – right." Benji passed the clips to Spike, who used them to fix the Maxileash to the bolts.

"That's that." Spike straightened up and dusted himself off, just as his dogtooth radio barked a message.

"Yapper to Spike!" Yapper's voice was faint with distance. *"Murdoch's calling in. He and Rascal are on the ship."*

DIDN'T GET NO CHANCE TO PLAY. SCAREDY CATS ALL RUN AWAY.
HE'S RIGHT. THE CATS GOT OFF THE *DONTPANIC* AS SOON AS THEY SAW US COMING. THEY'RE ESCAPING IN THEIR KATAMARAN.

"You'll get it," said Spike confidently. "No worries, leave everything to me. The Maxileash is fixed, I'm preparing to fire it right now." He ended the call.

Benji shifted from paw to paw in excitement. "What shall I do?"

Spike gave him a scornful look. "You? You can stay out of the way and don't touch anything. This is a delicate operation. The last thing we need is for some clumsy mutt to make a stupid mistake and ruin everything."

With those words, Spike turned away, tripped over his tool kit, and...

With a howl of despair, Benji picked up Spike's dogtooth radio. "Sally," he called, "Sally! It's Spike. He fell over and knocked himself out. What do I do?"

After a pause, he heard Sally's reply. "*Listen, Benji. I have to fly the Bonecopter. I can't leave the controls. And I can't land on the island, it's too rocky. I'm sorry, but there's only one thing for it.*"

Spike was still out cold. Everything depended on Benji now. "I can't do it!" he wailed.

"Of course you can," said Sally soothingly. *"Remember how good your aim was with the basketball? And the frisbee? You're a natural."*

"But this isn't a game!" howled Benji. "If I miss this time, it'll be a disaster!"

"Listen, Benji. All you have to do is hit the ship with the magnetic grab of the Maxileash. That will turn the Dontpanic *away from Sandy Banks and everyone will be saved. I have faith in you."*

Benji panted hard as his paw tightened on the trigger of the Maxileash.

The *Dontpanic* appeared in the Maxileash's sights. "I can see the sh-sh-ship," stammered Benji.

Sally's reply came over the radio. *"Don't panic."*

"Yes," said Benji crossly, "I know what it's called."

"No," said Sally patiently, *"I was just giving you some advice. Don't panic."*

"Oh. Right."

Benji felt giddy. He fumbled with the Maxileash's controls and checked the sights again. The magnetic grab seemed to be pointing right, but how could he be sure? If he missed...

"Remember not to snatch at the trigger," said Sally's voice. *"Ease it gently."*

Benji steeled himself. He could only do his best. "Oh, well," he muttered, "here goes nothing..."

He pulled the trigger.

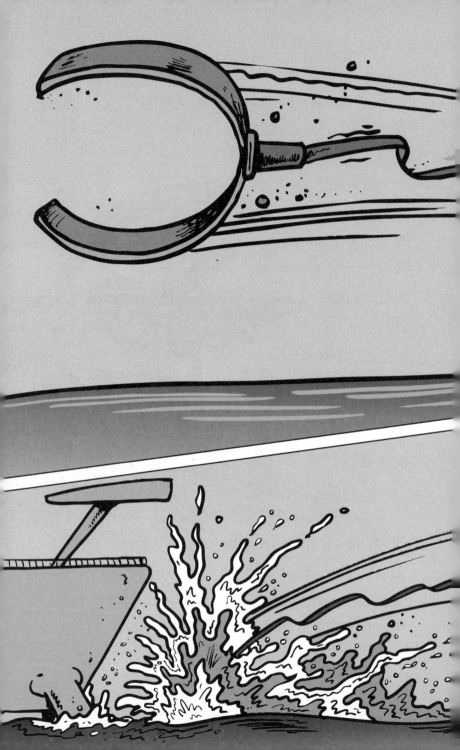

Sally's voice was calm. *"Take it easy, Benji. You forgot the ship was moving. You need to aim just ahead of it; and a little bit high."*

"But I missed!" whined Benji. "It's too late."

"The grab is on a line," Sally told him. *"All you have to do is wind in the line, and try again."*

"Oh – yeah, sure." Benji pressed a button on the Maxileash control board, and the line quickly wound back, hissing like a snake.

"Listen, Benji." Sally's voice was serious. *"The Dontpanic will be out of range soon. You'll only get one more chance. As soon as the line is wound in, you'll have to try again."* Benji whimpered. *"You can do it, Benji. I have faith in you."*

The grab appeared, dragging through the bushes lower down the hill, and slid back to Benji's feet.

Benji pulled himself together. This was the last chance – the very last chance. What was it Sally

had said? Aim just ahead of the ship and a little bit high. Benji spun the controls to point the Maxileash in the right direction. The ship was speeding away from him. It was now or never.

Once more, he pulled the trigger.

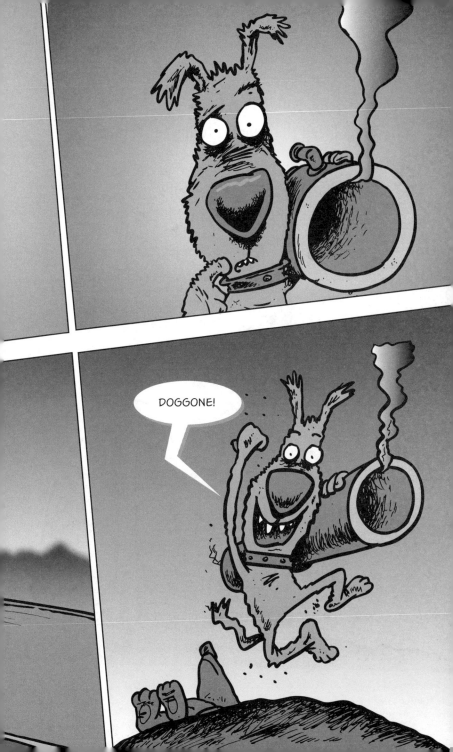

Sally's excited voice sounded from the dogtooth radio. *"Benji, you did it!"*

Benji lifted the headset to his ear. "I guess I did," he said in a dazed voice.

"The ship's turning," called Sally.

"Yeah, but..." Benji gave the Maxileash a worried look. "Uh-oh."

Benji groaned as Sally's voice echoed from the radio. *"Now you tell us!"*

"Ach, dinnae bother me now! I'm up to my neck in a nuclear reactor!"

Benji held his breath as the Maxileash strained against the force of the ship's engines. The

Dontpanic continued to come around the island. Benji crossed his paws. It looked as though his plan would work.

But just before the turn was complete...

Benji stared in horror as the line went slack. He yelped desperately into the radio. "Sally! Sally, the ship just broke free!"

"I just worked out the ship's new course," Sally continued. "The Maxileash turned her just enough. She'll miss Sandy Banks – she's heading out to sea. Murdoch and Rascal will have plenty of time to shut down the engines now."

Benji let out his breath with a whoosh. "Thank goodness for that. F.I.F.A."

Sally laughed. *"That's F.I.D.O., Benji."*

"Whatever," said Benji. Then he collapsed in a heap.

As Benji reeled in the line from the Maxileash and Sally brought the Bonecopter back to hover over the island, Spike opened his eyes.

WHAT? WHY? WHEN? WHERE? HOW?

Benji helped Spike to his feet. Spike looked around, blinking. "Who was playing football with my head?" Then he pulled himself together. "The ship!" he barked. "We must save the ship!"

"Um..." Benji gave him an apologetic look. "I guess I took care of that."

Spike stared at him. "You?"

"*Hey, boys!*" Sally was using the Bonecopter's loudhailer. "*I don't want to hurry you, but while you're catching up down there, Katmanchew's cats are escaping in their katamaran.*"

"Right!" snapped Spike. "Send down the winch." He started unfastening the clips that held the Maxileash to the rock.

SHOULDN'T WE LEAVE THAT AND GO AFTER THE CATS?

Spike gave him a hard look. "Listen, short stuff," he said, "it sounds like you did good today. But I'm still in charge here. Now help me get this back to the Bonecopter – we're going to need it if we want to stop Captain Claw's gang."

"Sure." Shamefaced, Benji hurried to obey.

A few minutes later, the Maxileash was safely back in the equipment bay on board the Bonecopter. Benji and Spike joined Sally in the cockpit as she turned the Bonecopter away from the island and set off after the fleeing felines.

Benji gave a yap of excitement and pointed.
"There they are!"

Spike smiled grimly. "Let's go put the cats out!"

Katmanchew hissed angrily as Captain Claw's face appeared on his communications screen. "What is it now, fool?"

GREAT MASTER – THE ACTION DOGS HAVE FOUND US!

"What?!" The crime lord's paws smashed down on the arms of his throne like hammers. "Mindless oaf! You told me the plan was working!"

"But it was!" howled Captain Claw.

Katmanchew's fangs gleamed. "And yet, my tracking stations have recorded no explosion. It seems the *Dontpanic* has not been destroyed – and now you're telling me you let the Action Dogs escape?"

"We did just as you told us, master," moaned Captain Claw.

"Blockhead!" raged Katmanchew. "Do I have to think of everything? Your boat is armed, is it not? Why do you think you have a katapult on board? Use it, you nincompuss!

"Blow the Action Dogs out of the sky!"

Sally frowned as aerial bombs from the katapult began to burst around the Bonecopter, causing it to rock wildly.

"Don't worry," said Spike, "I know how to fix them. Take us over the katamaran and open the equipment bay door."

A big grin spread over Benji's face. "Oh, I get it. That's why you wanted the Maxileash, right?"

"It works on big ships," said Spike grimly, "so I guess it should work on an itty-bitty boat."

Sally chuckled. "Go get 'em, boys!"

When Murdoch and Rascal returned in the *Dog Paddle*, they found a party in full swing.

"Murdoch, you're brilliant!" said Sally. "I knew you could shut down the *Dontpanic*'s engines."

"No problemo," drawled Rascal. "Did just fine. Took those babies way offline."

"Aye," said Murdoch, "but we couldnae have done it without help." He thrust his paw towards Benji.

"It looks as if everything has turned out all right," said Janet happily. "Sandy Banks is saved, the *Dontpanic* is being towed back into port for repairs. The passengers are even getting their valuables back from the katamaran. And Captain Claw and his motley crew are behind bars."

"And," said Sally, "isn't there something you want to say, Spike?"

"Er – yes." Spike coughed. He turned to Benji. "I thought you were just a dogsbody. It looks like Sally was right, and I was wrong. You came through for us today. So I had this made up for you."

WELCOME TO THE ACTION DOGS

Benji was so excited, it took several minutes to get him into his new uniform. But at last he was ready. In the meantime, Janet had set up a camera with an autotimer.

"Group photo, guys," she called. "Another mission successfully completed." She set the timer and scurried across to join her canine friends.

"You know," said Sally, "I have this weird feeling that it won't be long before we get another chance to unleash the..."

ACTION DOGS

NEXT TIME:

WILL THE

ACTION DOGS

SURVIVE...

THE HOWLING INFERNO

The Action Dogs are called to deal with a disastrous blaze that threatens the grand opening of the Van der Hund museum. Little do they know that the villainous feline Katmanchew and ninja spy Nikitty have put a dastardly scheme into action... Soon our heroes are trapped in a basement – and the air is running out!

ISBN 9781409520320

OUT NOW!

DANGER ON THE ICE

A sudden katastrophic rise in temperature at the South Pole has caused ice sheets to break up, stranding a team of scientists. Only one feline felon could be to blame...

Aboard the Sea Dog, it's full steam ahead for the Action Dogs to save the day. But with sea levels rising, and Katmanchew up to his old tricks, will the Action Dogs sink or swim...?

ISBN 9781409520337

TERROR IN SPACE

The conniving Katmanchew has set a spaceship on a collision course with a brand-new Space Hotel full of super-rich celebrities. Its time for the Action Dogs to blast off to the rescue in the Dog Starship! But Welfare Officer Brick is inspecting the pound – so it looks like the Action Dogs are firmly grounded.

Can the Dogs escape in time to stop a cosmic catastrophe, or will it all blow up in their faces...?

ISBN 9781409520344

THE DOGGY DIGGER

GRAB A PENCIL AND DESIGN YOUR OWN INDISPENSABLE ACTION DOGS GADGET! AND WHY NOT SCAN IT IN AND UPLOAD IT TO THE ACTION DOGS WEBSITE TOO?

Find out more about the 2 Steves at
WWW.THE2STEVES.NET

And for more fun reads than you can
shake a cat at, check out
WWW.FICTION.USBORNE.COM

First published in the UK in 2012 by Usborne Publishing Ltd., Usborne House, 83-85 Saffron Hill, London EC1N 8RT, England. www.usborne.com

A CIP catalogue record for this book is available from the British Library.

ISBN 9781409520191 JF AMJJASOND/12 00491/1
Printed in Dongguan, Guangdong, China.